THE MUMMY AWAKES

BULLSEYE CHILLERS

THE MUMMY AWAKES

By Megan Stine and
H. William Stine

Illustrated by Peter Peebles

BULLSEYE CHILLERS™

RANDOM HOUSE 🏠 NEW YORK

To Jenny Fanelli
For her great sense of humor and editorial finesse

A BULLSEYE BOOK PUBLISHED BY RANDOM HOUSE, INC.

Text copyright © 1993 by Megan Stine and H. William Stine.
Illustrations copyright © 1993 by Peter Peebles.
All right reserved under International and Pan-American Copyright
Conventions. Published in the United States by Random House, Inc.,
New York, and simultaneously in Canada by Random House of Canada
Limited, Toronto.

Library of Congress Cataloging-in-Publication Data:
Stine, Megan. The mummy awakes / by Megan Stine & H. William Stine.
    p.   cm. — (Bullseye chillers)
SUMMARY: Eleven-year-old Cameron Ross accidentally awakens the
mummy of a murdered Egyptian boy and finds that the mummy wants
to murder him.
ISBN 0-679-84193-8 (pbk.)   [1. Mummies—Fiction.   2. Horror stories.]
I. Stine, H. William.   II. Title.   III. Series.   PZ7.S86035Mq   1993
92-47288

Manufactured in the United States of America   10 9 8 7 6 5 4 3 2 1

Chapter 1

The night my mother came home from Egypt was the worst night of my life. Everything started then— the nightmares, the terror, and the mummy's horrible hold on me. From that night on, I knew the mummy wanted me dead.

It all began in early October. My mom called from the airport to say she was home. She'd been gone for six long weeks. I'd been staying with the people who lived in the apartment above ours. Now that my mom was back, I couldn't wait to see her. But she was going straight to the museum instead of coming home.

So I ran all the way in the rain to meet her. That's where my mom works—in the museum. It's just six blocks from our apartment in the city. When I finally found her, she was in the workroom deep in the basement. She was still wearing her raincoat, and was just about to pry open two large wooden crates.

My mom is an Egyptologist. She studies what Egypt was like three thousand years ago. Sometimes she goes away for months. She digs around in Egyptian caves and tombs, looking for mummies. Mummies are dead bodies, but they're all dried out so they don't rot. Most of the time they turn out to be kings and queens.

My mom's kind of famous because a few years ago she found three mummies. They're all here in the museum. They were lying on tables when I came in. They looked like corpses. Or people who were going to have surgery.

My mom loves looking at them and touching them. Not me. I think it's creepy to touch a dead body—even one that's three thousand years old. Oh, sure, the bodies are usually wrapped in old dirty cloth bandages. But sometimes my mom unwraps them. Then you get to see what the mummy really looks like.

None of them have eyes. Their noses are flat or broken. Their mouths gape open because their lips crumbled away centuries ago. And their bodies are all shrunken and bony. But the worst part is their skin—what's left of it. It's like tough, dark, wrinkled leather.

"Cameron!" my mom said when I walked into the workroom. She gave me a quick hug.

I was dying to tell her all the good stuff that had happened while she

was gone. But I didn't want to talk there, not in that room. Sometimes I got the crazy feeling that her mummies were listening.

Besides, my mom never paid much

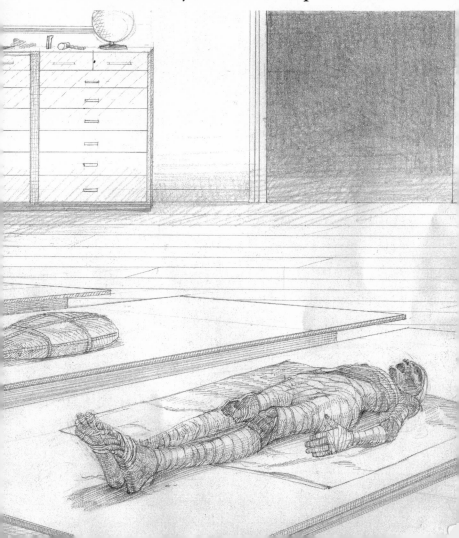

attention to me when she was working. Maybe that's why I really didn't like Egyptian stuff very much.

"Let me look at you," my mom said. She always talked quietly when the mummies were there, as if she thought they were just napping. "I think you've grown at least eight inches," she told me with a laugh.

I'm eleven years old. But I *am* pretty tall already, probably because of my dad. He was really tall. I have his black hair. But I have my mom's blue eyes. My dad died when I was four.

"Cameron, I've found wonderful things," she said. "Wait a minute. I'll show you." Then she turned to take things out of the crates.

I walked around the room. On one table lay the hideous mummy of a great Egyptian queen named

Meryt. On another table was a baby-size mummy that was found in Queen Meryt's tomb.

But the worst one was on the third table. It was Neshi, the mummy of a young boy, and I liked him the least. Maybe it was because he was around my age and size. Or maybe it was because he had been murdered. I don't know. All I knew was that I hated him. The back of his head was bashed in. His face and teeth looked like he wanted to bite someone—or scream.

"I found a number of important artifacts," my mom said as she pulled out pieces of bowls and plates and jewelry. They were tightly packed in shredded paper. Then she reached deep into the crate. "But look at these two treasures."

She unwrapped a short wooden

staff and handed it to me. It felt heavy and gritty from collecting three thousand years of dust. But I knew what it was. It was called a crook. It looked like a short shepherd's staff. At one end, the handle was curved like a question mark.

Then she put something else in my hand—another stick with loose strips of wood and leather at the end. It looked like a whip, but it was called a flail. It was used in harvesting crops.

I had seen both of them in my mom's books of ancient tomb paintings. The Egyptian kings—they were called pharaohs—carried the crook and the flail across their chest. They were both symbols of the pharaoh's power. The crook meant that the pharaoh was like a shepherd. He would protect his people. The flail

meant that he had the power to pun-
ish them, too.

"Cameron," my mom said. "If I
read the hieroglyphs in the tomb
correctly, these are the crook and
flail of the king who came after

Queen Meryt. Isn't that exciting?"

Oh yeah, Mom, I thought. Hiero-glyphs are a ton of excitement. They were little pictures of birds and scrolls and stuff. The Egyptians used them for writing words. But you had to be a genius to figure out what they meant.

My mom turned around again to open the second crate.

When she wasn't looking, I picked up the crook and flail. I waved them over Neshi.

I am more powerful than you are, I thought to myself. Then I folded my arms and crossed them over my chest, just as the pharaohs did.

Suddenly, before I knew what was happening, a hand reached out to stop me. I froze and looked down. Neshi's bony, half-wrapped hand was holding my wrist! My breathing stopped. I couldn't believe it. He was trying to get me to drop the crook. And he was squeezing so hard, I thought my wrist would shatter!

Chapter 2

I tried to scream. I tried to breathe. I tried to pull my arm away.

But I couldn't. My heart was pounding so wildly in my chest, I thought it would explode. The mummy was *alive!* His grip was like steel. And it felt like he was trying to rip my whole arm off!

Help me, Mom, I pleaded in my mind. Make him stop.

My fingers were turning numb because the mummy's grasp was shutting off the blood flow. Suddenly the crook slipped from my hand. It clattered loudly on the marble floor.

My mother whirled around in surprise and stared at me.

"Cameron!" she said. She rushed toward me. "How could you drop that? It's priceless!" She knelt in front of me and picked up the crook.

"But, Mom," I sputtered. "I..." My words stopped as soon as I looked at my wrist.

What was going on? The mummy wasn't holding on to me anymore! I looked over at Neshi. He was lying motionless on the table next to me. His hands were at his sides, just as they had been before.

My mother stood up and faced me. "Cameron, you *know* how priceless these things are," she said. "And they don't even belong to me. They're just on loan from the Egyptian government. Your carelessness could have destroyed them!"

"Mom, I couldn't help it," I said. My whole body was trembling. "I *had* to drop it. He made me. He grabbed my wrist!"

She looked at me strangely. "Cameron," she said with surprise. "What's the matter with you? You never make up stories."

"I'm *not* making it up, Mom!" I said. "I know it sounds crazy, but that mummy is alive! He moved!"

She sighed and shook her head. "It's late and I'm tired. We'll talk about this in the morning."

I knew what that meant. She didn't believe a word I had said. And I couldn't blame her. My story sounded *totally* crazy. But what could I do? It was the truth. My wrist was sore and bruised.

When we got home, my mom and I went straight to bed. We were both too tired to talk. And that's when the nightmare began.

It started with voices, voices in the dark. They were yelling, and I couldn't tell what they were saying. But they were angry, and I was afraid. First there were men's voices, then a boy's. His voice sounded a lot like mine.

The pictures in the dream were blurry. I couldn't see anything clearly, except for hands grabbing at a boy. I couldn't see his face. But he was my age, my size. And he had my black hair. In my heart, I knew it was me.

The boy screamed at the top of his lungs. He was trying to get away. I knew exactly how he felt. The same way I felt when I tried to get away from Neshi's grip.

Then I saw a hand with a large

rock. It was a bony brown hand. The hand swung down onto the back of the boy's head—my head—with a crunch.

No! I cried out in the dream. Don't hurt me! Then the boy fell forward silently. I never saw his face, but I knew he was dead.

I woke up with a jerk, terrified. I was soaking wet. I thought it was blood, but it was only sweat. The covers were twisted around my feet like ropes.

I sat up in bed, shaking with fear. And as soon as I was fully awake, I knew what the dream meant. It was a message from Neshi. For some reason—I didn't know why—the mummy wanted me dead!

Chapter 3

After I had that dream, I got a horrible, sick feeling in the pit of my stomach. It wouldn't go away.

So the next day, right after school, I went to the museum. I wanted to prove to myself that the dream was just a nightmare—nothing more.

It couldn't be true. Neshi couldn't kill me. Could he?

When I got there, he was still lying on a table in the basement room. My mom was studying the crook and flail. She was surprised to see me, since I didn't usually bother her at work. I tried to make up some reason why I had come, but my eyes kept looking over at the real reason. Then I saw Neshi's fingers begin to move, stretching slowly toward me.

Suddenly my legs buckled under me and I was on the floor. I almost fainted.

My mom came rushing over. "Cameron, are you feeling all right?"

I wanted to answer her. But what could I say? That the mummy *was* alive? That he just tried to grab me? I looked at Neshi. He was motionless. I had no proof.

I got up and ran out of the room as fast as I could. All the way home I asked myself, why? Why had I picked up the crook and flail? Why had I waved them over Neshi's mummy? What kind of ancient curse had I set off?

And why did I have to die?

I promised myself I'd never go back to the museum. Ever.

But the very next day, right after school, I went there again. I couldn't stop myself. I tried to go home, but instead I went to the museum. Somehow Neshi was making me come!

When I got there, I found that Neshi and the other mummies had been moved. I guess my mom was done working on them because now they were on display in the Ancient Egypt Room.

Neshi was the centerpiece. He was lying in his coffin, inside a glass display case in the middle of the room. Queen Meryt was in her own coffin, in a glass case near the wall. Lying next to her was the little mummy— the one that had been found in the queen's tomb.

The little mummy was really weird.

At first everyone thought it was Queen Meryt's baby. But when my mom X-rayed it, it turned out to be a baboon baby instead! No one knew why a baboon had been buried with the queen.

The crook and flail were hanging above them on the wall. My mom had put up a sign. It said that these objects probably belonged to the pharaoh who came after the queen. All the other walls were covered with ancient Egyptian writings and paintings.

The room was sort of dark and airless. It felt closed in, like a tomb.

But I stood there for hours anyway, staring at Neshi. Every so often a security guard wandered through the room and gave me a strange look.

But I didn't care. I was waiting for

Neshi to move. I looked at him, still and silent in his heavy wooden coffin. I watched his lipless mouth, waiting for it to smile at me. His empty eye sockets looked straight back at me, revealing nothing. But even with the half-inch-glass display case between us, I still didn't feel safe.

Nothing happened—until closing time. That was the first time I was totally alone with Neshi. All the museum visitors had gone, and the place was silent. Then I saw the mummy's fingers begin to twitch, just a little.

I wanted to scream, "Look, somebody! Neshi is alive!"

But I didn't scream. How could I? Nobody saw him move but me. People would think I was nuts. So I kept it all inside. And every day after school, I went back for more.

Going to the museum was like a

curse of its own. I didn't want to go. And when I got to the museum, I tried to leave. But somehow Neshi was holding me there. Only after I'd been in his presence for several hours did I feel free to leave.

My friends started getting mad. Especially Ben, my best friend. I never wanted to be with him anymore. I even cut school and stopped doing my homework. Nothing mattered to me except the mummy.

When I was with Neshi, I tried communicating with him through my mind. Why do you want to kill me? I'd think over and over. What did I do to you?

But the mummy never answered me. Not in the daytime, anyway.

At night, though, every night, I had the same terrible dream—the dream about my own death!

Chapter 4

The nightmares went on for two solid weeks. Each morning, I woke up more tired than ever. I felt like I hadn't slept at all. The tension was wearing me down.

My mom started to get mad. She saw that I was a wreck. But she thought it was all my fault—that I was staying up late reading comic books or something.

So one night at dinner, I tried to explain what was wrong. I told her all about the nightmare. But I didn't tell her that Neshi was alive. I knew she wouldn't believe that.

Afterward, she squinted at me. "Cameron," she said. "Are you having trouble at school? Or trouble with your friends, maybe? Or have you been watching too many horror movies?" She was looking for some way to explain the nightmares.

"It's nothing like that," I said. I *knew* she wouldn't understand. "It's Neshi."

"Neshi?"

"Yes. I think he wants me dead."

Believe it or not, she smiled when I said that! She actually thought it was funny.

"Neshi is a mystery, Cameron," she said, still smiling. "I agree with that. But he doesn't want you dead. How could he? He's not even alive himself."

That's what you think, Mom, I thought to myself. But all I said was, "Tell me more about him."

She plunged right in. My mom was always thrilled to talk about her mummies.

"Well, there is a bit of writing carved *inside* his coffin, which is unusual. But the writing doesn't tell us much," she said. "All I know is that he was not royalty. Still, he should have had a Book of the Dead in his tomb. But I never found one."

"What's that?" I asked.

"It's a scroll that was usually buried with a mummy. It had charms and magical spells to help the mummy in his life after death."

She'd told me about this stuff before. The Egyptians believed that a person's spirit lived on after death. But you had to have a body for the spirit to live in. That's why they mummified people. They dried out the body with salts and then stuffed it. The mummy was a resting place for the soul.

"Why are you so interested in Neshi these days?" my mom asked.

"I told you, Mom. Because he's going to kill me," I said.

She sighed. "I don't understand you, Cameron Ross," she said.

I hated it when she used my last name.

"You know what the trouble with

you is, Mom?" I said as I stomped out of the room. "You don't understand *anything* unless it's written in hiero-glyphs!"

Actually, I thought that was a pretty good line. And I didn't care if it hurt her feelings. I was mad. Couldn't she see that I was having the worst experience of my life? That I felt totally alone?

The next day after school, my friend Ben caught up with me. I was on my way to the museum.

"Hey, Cam, wait!" Ben called. He was moving slowly under the weight of his backpack. I guess we had a lot of homework that day. But I didn't care. I had left all my books at school.

"We've gotta talk," he said, push-ing his brown hair back. Ben's hair always hung down over his wire-rimmed glasses. He was about four inches shorter than me, but he didn't look like a shrimp. He just hadn't had his growth spurt yet.

"I can't talk now," I said.

"Oh, right. You have to go to the museum," he said. "And don't tell me you're helping your mom because I called the other day. She told me the truth—that you just go to the museum and stare at a mummy. Why are you doing that?"

I shrugged my shoulders. I wanted to tell him, but I couldn't. Living mummies, curses, vengeance—Ben hated stuff like that. He thought it was too dumb to be true.

We just looked at each other for a minute. Then I started to walk away. I wanted to stay and talk, but I couldn't. Neshi was pulling me toward him.

"Hey, you're coming to my birth-day party on Saturday, aren't you?" Ben called. "Come early and we'll do something cool—like put pepper in my little brother's cupcake."

Maybe he read my mind. Or maybe he just read the look on my

face. But suddenly he knew.

"You're not coming, are you?" Ben said. He threw his backpack on the ground. "I don't believe it. You're skipping my party so you can go see that mummy instead! Are you nuts?"

I just shrugged.

"Listen," Ben yelled, "if you don't come to my party, our friendship is over. Get it?"

I got it.

Then he grabbed his backpack and walked away.

Chapter 5

"Hey, my man, Cameron," said Malcolm.

I looked up and saw my favorite security guard on his way through the Ancient Egypt Room. Malcolm was tall and dark, with black hair and long arms and legs. He was from Jamaica.

"What's new with your skinny buddy?" He knocked on Neshi's glass case and laughed. "He sit up and say hi to you yet?"

"No," I said. I didn't mind when Malcolm teased me. He had a great smile, so I always knew he was being funny, not mean.

Malcolm's face turned serious. "You've been coming here every day for three weeks, Cameron," he said. "Why do you like this stuff so much?"

"I'm working on a special school project," I lied.

"Uh-huh," Malcolm said quietly. "I still think you should be out playing somewhere. Whatever happened to that friend of yours—the short kid with the glasses?"

"Who, Ben?" I turned my head away. "Ben and I aren't friends anymore," I said. "I didn't go to his birthday party last Saturday, and that was that."

"A guy needs friends," Malcolm said. He checked his watch. It was time to finish his rounds in the museum.

When he was gone, when the

squeak of his shoes on the marble floor disappeared, I moved closer to Neshi. A guy doesn't need friends if he's going to get his head smashed in, I said to myself. I stared into the glass case at the small leathery boy lying there. I saw his thin fingers begin to twitch again.

Suddenly a hand clamped down on my shoulder. I screamed and jerked away.

"Hey, don't make so much noise. You'll wake the dead!" said Ben's voice behind me.

I turned around.

"What are you doing here?" I asked.

"I came to tell you we're still friends," Ben said. "Even if you didn't come to my party. Okay?"

I had almost forgotten how to smile. "Okay," I told Ben.

"Great. Let's get out of here," he said.

When he said that, my heart started to pound faster. "I can't," I said. "I've got to stay."

"Why?" Ben asked.

"Because this mummy wants to kill me," I said. "So I've got to watch him."

I could see that Ben thought I was being a jerk. But he stayed calm. "Okay, let's say you're right," he said. "Let's say Mr. Bandage Buddy here wants to kill you. How's he going to get you?"

"I don't know," I had to admit.

"What's he going to do?" Ben went on. "Smash his way out? I mean, be logical, Cam. Look at his hands. Those bones are three thousand years old. What do you think is going to break when that hand smashes into half an inch of safety glass?"

In my heart I knew Ben was totally and completely wrong. I knew Neshi was dangerous. I knew I shouldn't leave that room. But I wanted to believe him. I wanted to leave the museum and go be myself again.

"Okay," I said. "Let's go." At least if I went somewhere with Ben, maybe I could stop thinking about Neshi for a while.

It was almost time for the museum to close. The place was eerily empty as we walked to the main door. I stopped in the arched doorway and looked down the stone steps. The air felt chilly outside, and strange. The moon was already high in the dark sky. It seemed like the kind of night when werewolves would be on the prowl—if they existed. Halloween was only a few days away.

Ben and I ran down the steps. As the traffic light changed, he raced across the street. He was heading into the park across from the museum.

"Wait!" I yelled, running after him. Why did he have to take the shortcut home tonight? It was only two blocks shorter. And it was so much darker—and creepier.

Sure, there were streetlights dotting the cement walkways in the park. But even with the lights and a sliver of the moon, I couldn't see very far ahead on the path. And for sure I couldn't see what was lurking in the trees.

I was out of breath when I caught up with him.

"Ben—" I started to say. But I stopped. Ben stopped walking and turned around.

"What was that?" he said. He

swiped at his hair, pushing it away from his glasses.

I froze. There were sounds behind us. Like footsteps. Except more of a shuffling sound. I was too terrified to even turn around and look.

"Did you hear that?" Ben asked.

I nodded. Of course I heard it. And I knew what it was.

"The mummy is following us!" I told him. And the sick feeling returned to my stomach.

Chapter 6

I listened carefully to the sounds in
the trees. The slow, dragging footsteps were first on one side of us,
then the other. They were shuffling
closer and closer all the time.

"Let's go," I said, pulling Ben's
arm. "Now."

"Maybe it's the wind," Ben said un-
certainly. "We heard the wind."

"It was Neshi," I insisted. "He's
following me. Every second he's
coming closer."

When I said that, Ben shook
his head. He wouldn't believe in
a living mummy, no matter how

many footsteps he heard.

I started to run, but Ben tackled me. We rolled in the dirt near the edge of a hill. Down the hill below us was a ravine that ran through the park. Ben ended up sitting on my chest.

"Now listen!" he yelled at me. "Mummies don't walk through parks at night. They don't control people's minds. They just lie there and stink!"

"They don't stink," I said. "Don't you know anything?" Ben was heavy on my chest. "Get off me."

"No. Not until you tell me you're going to stop going to the museum. I mean it, Cam. I'm your friend, so I've got to keep you away from that mummy. He's messing up your head."

I didn't say anything. I saw flashes of white bandages behind Ben in the trees. Neshi was there. I could feel it. I could almost hear him talking to me.

Ben looked around nervously. He felt it too.

"Let me up," I said desperately.

Finally, Ben moved. We both stood up, staring into the darkness.

"I don't hear anything, do you?" Ben asked. "There's nothing there."

I turned in a circle, listening and watching the trees. "No," I said. "I don't hear anything. But I know he's still there."

Ben let out a long breath and almost shivered. I could tell he was almost as scared as I was. But he was trying to act tough.

I walked to the edge of the hill and pulled my denim jacket tight around me. All of a sudden my head snapped up. There it was again—

that shuffling sound behind us!

I whirled around just in time to see a white blur coming toward me. Oh, no! I thought. This is it. He's going to kill me!

He was there, the mummy, his linen wrappings trailing in the wind. And then in a blink he was gone.

In the next instant, Ben screamed and went flying past me, stumbling on his feet. I reached out, but I couldn't catch him in time.

He fell forward, over the edge of the hill, into the ravine. He was yelling the whole way down. When he finally crashed, the night was deadly silent.

Chapter 7

I stood frozen at the edge of the hill.

"Ben!" I yelled down to him. There was no answer. So I started down the hill. But it was steeper than I had thought. I slid and fell until I reached him. He was lying on the ground, not moving.

"Ben," I said. "Are you okay?"

Finally he sat up. "Yeah, I guess," he said. "But I hurt all over." I helped him to his feet. "Who pushed me?" he asked.

"It was the mummy," I said. "Neshi tried to kill you. Didn't you see?"

"I didn't see anything," Ben said. "I felt two hands push me and that's all."

Well, *I* saw him. Maybe not for long, but long enough. I knew Neshi had pushed Ben. How did he get out of the museum? Did he smash his way out—like Ben said he couldn't? Or could he just move right through glass and walls? My mind thumped with a million questions.

But the biggest question was this: It was me he wanted to kill. And he'd had a chance! Why hurt Ben?

We walked home in silence, taking the long way. Not through the park. When we got to Ben's, I stayed there as long as I could. But finally I had to leave—alone. I walked home, looking over my shoulder the whole way.

The small elevator in our building was empty. I had never been afraid to ride the elevator alone before, but I was now.

When I got to my floor, I hurried into our apartment. My mom was curled up in her big, soft blue chair. With the matching footstool, it practically filled the living room.

She barely moved at all when she saw me. "We've got to talk," she said. "Where've you been, Cameron?"

"You won't like it," I warned. I knew she'd think I was lying, but I told her the truth anyway. About Neshi pushing Ben. Of course I was right. She didn't believe a word I said. *Nobody* did. Why should they? It sounded too impossible to be true.

"Cameron, I know how interested in Neshi you've become," she said. Her voice was getting shaky, and tears were coming to her eyes. "Now I have to ask you something. Did you...did you for some reason steal Neshi from the museum tonight?"

"Are you nuts?" I yelled.

"All I want is for you to tell me the truth, Cameron," she said. "I know you have the security code to the museum's back door."

I stared at her, not saying anything. How could she think I would do a thing like that? As if to answer me, she held out her hand.

"Look at this," she said.

My mom put a small piece of stiff cloth into my open hand. "I found this in your room tonight," she said. "You know what it is, don't you? It's a scrap of linen. A piece of Neshi's wrappings."

I dropped it as if it were burning my hand. "Oh, no," I moaned. "That means he knows where I live. He's been in my room!"

"This is very serious, Cameron," she said. "Someone broke into the museum tonight. They smashed the display case and stole Neshi."

I felt a horrible panic. "He's not stolen, Mom. He broke out. And he's coming to get me."

My mom's head dropped, and she sighed. "Just go to your room," she said. "We'll talk about this when you're ready to say something real."

I didn't want to go to my room. I wanted to run for about a million miles. But would I really be safe even then?

Tears filled my eyes as I went down the hall. I flopped down on my bed and prayed with all my heart that the mummy wouldn't come back. At least not tonight.

But a minute later I jumped up again. My bed was too soft and warm and I definitely didn't want to fall asleep. How many times could I watch myself being killed in that horrible dream?

I sat down in the straight-backed chair at my desk, knowing I could never fall asleep there.

A minute later, my head dropped onto the desk.

The dream started instantly.

I saw myself struggling in the arms of strong men. The dream was still blurry, and I couldn't see my own face. But somehow I could see more than before.

No! Get back! Let me go! Now there were *two* men. Or was it three? Here comes the bony brown hand with the rock....

The back of my head ached, waiting for the rock to smash and kill me.

But suddenly there was something I had never seen before. It was the crook and flail—the same ones my mom had brought home from

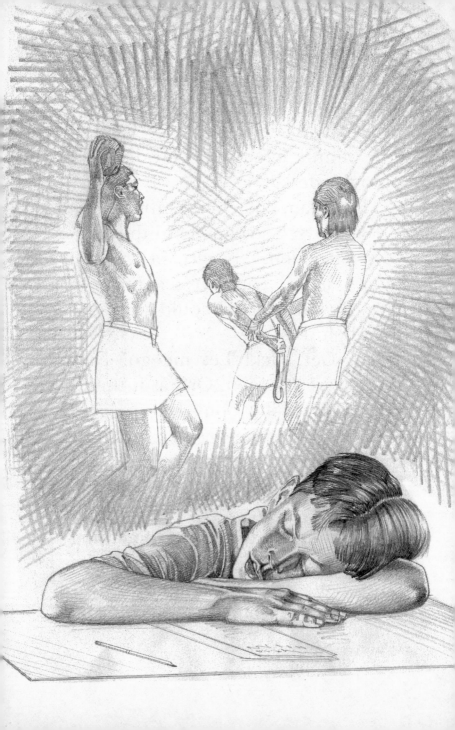

Egypt! The boy—it had to be me—I was holding them and screaming for my life.

"Aghhhhhhh!" Then the screams stopped, and everything went blood red.

I jerked awake so fast that I fell off the chair onto my bedroom floor. I pulled my knees up to my chin and sat there trembling. Now I understood why I had to die. In the dream, I was holding the crook and flail, the ancient symbols of power. But the men knew I was a faker! I was only pretending to be a prince.

And that's what I had done in real life. I had picked up the crook and flail and waved them over Neshi. I had pretended to be a prince! That's why Neshi wanted me dead.

Chapter 8

"Sorry, Cam, but I have to work late tonight." My mom dropped this bombshell the next morning at breakfast. "So you'll be alone, probably till midnight."

She kept talking about other stuff. Something about me being grounded if I went near the museum again. But I wasn't listening. All I could think about was Neshi. He had come looking for me last night. And I knew he'd keep coming back until he found me.

That's when I came up with a brilliant plan—for a sleepover with Ben,

Carlos, and Adam. They would be my protection.

My mom loved it. She even smiled. "I'm glad you want to see your friends again," she said. "Now maybe you can stop thinking about the mummy."

"What mummy?" I said cheerfully. She didn't know I was faking. My whole face was a total lie.

That night I walked around the living room waiting for the guys to show up. Then I got a can of soda in the kitchen. Right before I popped the can, I heard a noise. I didn't know what it was, but I was pretty sure it came from my bedroom.

Was it Neshi? Had he come for me already? I walked slowly toward my room. But before I got there, the doorbell rang. I jumped a little. Then I laughed at myself and raced back to the front hall.

"Who is it?" I called through the door.

"Santa Claus," said Ben. "Open up. Do we need a security check or something?"

As fast as I could, I unlocked the two locks on the door and unfastened the chain. Carlos, Adam, and Ben were standing there.

"Par-ty! Par-ty!" the three of them chanted, pushing their way past me and dropping their sleeping bags in the living room.

"I brought some baseball cards you can't live without, Cam-man," Carlos said with a laugh. Carlos thought he was a pretty slick salesman. "Let's go talk trades."

Trades? I didn't want to trade baseball cards. All my cards were in my room. What if that sound I heard was Neshi? "Uh, hey—wait, you guys," I said.

But they were already in my room. I listened a minute. No one was screaming. I figured everything must be all right.

Hey, this plan is working out great, I thought. These guys *are* protecting me!

I hurried down the hall and joined my friends. Carlos had set up shop, spreading his baseball cards on my bed. And Adam was already going through my cards, picking out the ones he wanted me to trade.

"Hey, Cameron, where is it?" asked Adam. "Where's the card your dad gave you?"

"Forget it," I said quickly. "No way I'm trading that one."

"We just want to see it again," Ben said.

That was a special card. I kept it hidden in a special place, the bottom of my underwear drawer. It was a famous Cleveland Indians pitcher from the 1950s. My dad had gotten it when he was a kid.

I took out the card and gave it to Ben first. Ben stared at it for a minute. But just as he was passing it to Carlos, all the lights went out.

"What's the joke?" Carlos said.

"Hey, cool," Ben said. "It's a blackout!"

"Hide-and-seek in the dark!" Adam shouted. "Ben's it!"

In an instant they all scrambled out of my room. I heard their footsteps going down the hall into the dark apartment. But I had a better plan. I quietly crept toward my bedroom closet and stepped deep into the cool darkness. I almost had to laugh. No one would find me there for hours, I thought. A blackout, wow. That hadn't happened in years. Wasn't it weird that it happened tonight?

I heard the closet door open. It was still too dark for me to see anything.

"I don't believe it," I said. "Ben, how'd you know I was here?"

Ben didn't answer.

"Ben? Is that you?" I asked.

No answer.

"Carlos? Adam? Come on, you guys," I said.

Just then something incredibly strong clamped on to my wrist.

"Hey!" I said. I pushed him away with my free hand and touched something that felt like dry, brittle cloth. For an instant I froze in fear. I touched the arm. It was bony and hard. My heart was racing when I reached out and touched the face. But there was no face! Just a leathery skeleton head. It was Neshi, pulling me closer and closer to him!

I screamed for my life—just like in the dream. I screamed bloody murder as loud and as long as I could.

Chapter 9

When I couldn't scream anymore, I collapsed to the floor of the closet. My whole body was trembling with fear. Any minute I knew my head would be bashed in.

Someone grabbed both my arms and started shaking me. "Cam, what's your problem?" a voice yelled.

Suddenly the lights came on again. Ben, Carlos, and Adam were standing there. They were looking down at me as if I were an idiot.

I jumped to my feet and looked around my room. Neshi was nowhere in sight. I sat down on my bed.

"What's going on?" Ben asked. He sounded really worried.

"The mummy. In the closet. Tried to kill me," I said. My voice was thin. I was trying not to cry.

Carlos started to laugh. I knew he thought I was nuts.

"Hey, look at this," said Adam. He picked up a baseball card from the floor. It was my dad's special card.

"Oh, man! Look what happened to it!" Carlos said.

Ben and I stared at the card. I

started to shake again. There were hieroglyphs written right across the picture! Except they weren't written in ink. The marks looked like they'd been *burned* in.

"Who did it?" Ben asked.

"Who do you think?" I said. "The mummy."

He didn't want to believe it, but I could tell from his face that maybe he did.

"Man, he ruined your card," Carlos said. "What do all those marks mean?"

"I don't know," I said. "But it must be some kind of message. Like he's trying to tell me something. I'm going to the museum to find out what it means."

Ben looked worried. "Your mom said you couldn't go there."

"Yeah," I said. "But I've got a

signed permission slip—from a dead guy." I held up the baseball card with the markings on it. Ben gave a half smile. "You guys better stay here," I added. "I'll be back soon—I hope."

They didn't have any trouble agreeing to stay.

On the way to the museum I looked at the card again. I'd seen those symbols somewhere before. There were three of them. And there was an oval line drawn around the whole thing.

Hey, wait a minute, I thought. An oval around hieroglyphs? My mom had told me about that. It was called a cartouche. The names of kings and queens were written that way.

The museum was just closing when I got there. So the place was as quiet as a tomb. The guards were all stationed at the public exits. I slipped in a back door used only by people who worked there. It was easy because I knew the security code for that door's alarm.

But as soon as I got inside, I knew I was in trouble. There on the floor by the door was a shred of Neshi's wrappings! I was back on his turf, and I could feel he was nearby.

Well, I thought to myself. I've come this far. I'm going to find out why he wants me dead.

I hurried to the Ancient Egypt Room. There were hieroglyphs all over the place. On the walls, on artifacts, on the queen's coffin.

But all along I knew where the answer was. It had to be inside Neshi's coffin. I stared at the coffin for a moment before taking my first slow step toward it. The glass case Neshi had smashed was gone. Now there was just a red velvet rope around the empty coffin.

The heavy wooden lid had been propped up at an angle with a wooden stick. My mom thought it looked cool that way—as if the lid were on hinges, and it was just about to close.

I ducked under the rope and climbed inside. The coffin fit me perfectly—like it had been made for me.

I took a deep breath. Inside the box, there was a single row of tiny carved hieroglyphs. Of course the symbols I was looking for were there—the same ones as on the baseball card. Except that in the coffin, they weren't written in a cartouche.

As soon as I saw them, I remembered what they meant. They were the hieroglyphs for Neshi's name! My mom had pointed them out to

me when she first found Neshi. That
was years ago.

But what did his message mean? I
wondered. Why did he put his name
in a cartouche? Was he trying to tell
me he was a king or a prince—or—

Wait a minute! Was someone
coming? I thought I heard shuffling
footsteps.

SLAM!

The whole earth shook around me. Everything went black. The coffin lid had crashed down, sealing me in.

Right away, I could tell I was running out of air.

In a few minutes, I realized, this would be my coffin—forever!

Chapter 10

Panic took over. I rolled over on my back and screamed at the top of my lungs. Like a trapped animal, I kicked and pounded on the coffin lid. But the lid wouldn't move. And I knew why. Neshi was holding it down.

"Let me out of here!" I screamed. "Help!" But my screams didn't even sound loud to me. They were smothered by the tiny space and the heavy wooden box.

And anyway, who would hear me in an empty museum? I sobbed, gasping for air that was quickly running out. I didn't have much time.

My own sweat mixed with the coffin smells. I began to feel dizzy. I was fainting, maybe from fear, maybe from lack of oxygen. My eyelids grew heavy too.

And as soon as my eyes closed, the dream started again.

It was the same dream, but this time nothing was blurry. I saw everything clearly for the first time.

The boy. The three strong men. The bony brown hand. The rock.

But then suddenly I saw someone who had never been in the dream before. An old woman was following the men, pleading with them. They didn't listen to her. They pushed her to the ground.

I hadn't noticed it before, but everyone in the dream was dressed in Egyptian clothing.

Was that me—in ancient Egypt? Was *I* the king or prince?

Just then the boy fought and broke free! He rushed to the old woman, hugging her, clinging to her. And finally, for the first time, I saw his face!

It wasn't my face. It was Neshi! I knew because he looked like his mummy. But he looked better in the dream. He was alive!

A moment later he was murdered, as he had been every night in my dreams.

Then suddenly I was in a dark room, a tomb. This was a new part of the dream. In the middle of the room was Neshi's body. It was partially wrapped in linen bandages. He was being mummified.

From a dark passageway, the old woman appeared again. She was

creeping into the tomb. She stopped to make sure no one followed her.

She bent over the dead boy and kissed his cheek. Then suddenly she loosened some of the wrappings—and put something inside his mouth! It looked like a small piece of clay.

Next she loosened the wrappings around the boy's chest. She hid a scroll inside the mummy's bandages.

A sudden loud scraping of wood against wood woke me from my dream. The lid to the coffin was moving, slowly opening. All of my senses leaped awake. My body stiffened. This is it, I thought. Neshi's going to kill me now!

Chapter 11

The lid to the coffin lifted slowly, and I held my breath. Two eyes peered down at me over the edge of the coffin.

"My man, Cameron," said my friend Malcolm. "Don't you have a bedroom of your own to sleep in?"

I couldn't decide whether to laugh or cry or throw up. I wanted to do everything at once. "Malcolm!" I gasped. I took in big gulps of the room's cold air. "I thought I was going to die."

He gave me a hand out of the coffin. "You could have," he said.

"Lucky for you the motion detectors picked up the lid slamming down. Why'd you do it?"

"All of a sudden it just closed," I explained. There was no way he was going to believe what really happened—that Neshi locked me in. "Thanks for helping me. But I've got to find my mom."

I was still pretty shaky, so Malcolm walked with me down all the long, dark hallways and stairs to the workroom. My mom was sitting at a desk, looking at an ancient bowl under a magnifying glass.

"Mom!" I said, bursting into the room.

She wheeled her chair around. "Cameron, what on earth are you doing here?"

"Mom, I think I know something about Neshi," I said.

She looked at me and she looked at Malcolm. You'd think from her expression that I had just told her I was going to drop a bomb on Egypt.

"Mom, I know you don't want to hear this, but I had a dream and I saw things."

She tilted her head at me as if she were just a little bit curious. "What did you see?"

"I saw someone put a small piece of clay in Neshi's mouth. There's also a scroll in his bandages."

I took the baseball card out of my back jeans pocket. "And look, Mom," I went on. "Look what he did to Dad's card. He wrote his name in a cartouche. Don't you get it? He's saying that he's a prince or maybe even a king. And I'll bet the proof is on that piece of clay in his mouth."

My mom stood up and stared at the baseball card.

"Cameron, you wouldn't—" she started to say.

"No, Mom," I said. "You know I wouldn't. I'd never write on Dad's favorite card."

She smiled. She believed me! It seemed like the first time in weeks.

"Well," she said. "I never completely unwrapped Neshi. I was always afraid of damaging him. Too late now."

Just then Malcolm's walkie-talkie started squawking. "Any unit. This is Howard, requesting backup."

In a flash Malcolm had his walkie-talkie to his lips. "This is Malcolm. What's the problem?"

A worried voice came back over the speaker. "I heard footsteps going into Sector 23, and I followed them.

But I don't believe what I found. You'd better get here fast."

"Where's Sector 23?" I asked.

Malcolm answered me, but he was staring right at my mom. "It's the Ancient Egypt Room," he said.

Chapter 12

"This is impossible," my mother said, shaking her head.

We were all panting a little. We had run up three flights of stairs to the Ancient Egypt Room.

We stared at Neshi's coffin—the same coffin I had been lying in a few minutes before. Now Neshi was there! The mummy lay on his back, squeezed into his coffin as if he hadn't moved from there in three thousand years.

"I don't know how he got here unless he walked," said the guard who had called on the walkie-talkie.

No one laughed at his joke. Nothing was too strange to be true.

"Mom, are you going to look in his mouth?" I asked.

She quietly nodded and pulled a pair of tweezers from her lab jacket pocket. With one hand, she carefully removed a wad of sticky brown linen from Neshi's mouth. Then she shined a small light inside.

"There's something there. This is incredible!" With the small metal tweezers, she coaxed a thin oval piece of clay from Neshi's throat. "There's writing on it," she said, holding it under the brightest light in the room.

"What does it say, Mom?" I asked.

"It says, 'I am Prince Neshi, son of Queen Meryt'!" she answered.

"That's the message! He's been trying to tell us that he's a prince!"

After that, my mom sprang into action. She sent Malcolm to bring back a long folding work table. Then she loaded Neshi onto it so she could unwrap his bandages. Soon she reached between layers of the cloth and pulled out a scroll. It was made out of papyrus—an ancient Egyptian kind of paper.

"It's Neshi's Book of the Dead," she said, unrolling the scroll. "And his name is written here dozens of times. He's called *Prince* Neshi."

"Dr. Ross," Malcolm said. "You mean Neshi has been resting in the same room with his mother all these years and nobody knew it?"

My mom kept unrolling the scroll and shaking her head. Then she came to a loose piece of papyrus. "Here's a separate page," she said.

Her eyes moved across the symbols

at lightning speed. "It was written by a scribe who took down the words of an old woman named Herya. She was one of Queen Meryt's servants. Amazing…"

"What?" Malcolm and I both asked at the same time.

"Well," my mother said slowly. "This says the queen died in child-birth. But the child did not die! However, another woman wanted the child killed. That way, her own son could become pharaoh.

"So the other woman paid a lot of money to Herya to kill the queen's baby. But Herya couldn't do it. She gave the money to priests who mum-mified a baboon baby instead."

"Weird," I said. "So I guess every-one was supposed to think the ba-boon was the dead baby?"

My mother nodded. "Meanwhile,

the servant took Neshi far from the city and raised him as a prince. But when the other woman found out that Neshi was still alive, she sent soldiers to kill him. He was only twelve years old."

"They hit him from behind with a rock," I said.

"You're right," my mom said. "It was just like you told me. And you've solved the mystery of the baboon baby. That was something I've wondered about for years."

"It's because of the crook and flail, Mom," I said. I took them down from their display on the wall and carried them to Neshi's coffin. "I was playing with them, and Neshi grabbed my hand because they really belong to him."

"Grabbed your hand?" said my mom, tilting her head at me again.

"Yeah," I said. "But I think he was just trying to communicate with me. He wanted me to know he was a prince—and that the crook and flail were really his."

I was quiet for a minute, thinking back. "He probably pushed Ben in the park because Ben was trying to keep me away from the museum," I added. "And he trapped me in his coffin to make me have that dream."

"No, Cameron," my mother said firmly. "I don't know how Neshi got back here, or how those other things happened. But I do know one thing. Mummies don't come back to life."

My mom turned away then and started talking with the guards. Suddenly I got an idea. I put the crook in one of Neshi's hands and the flail in the other. That's where they belong, I thought to myself.

But then the most incredible thing happened. Neshi actually began to move. His fingers closed tightly around the crook and flail—just as they had closed around my wrist! Then he bent his arms until the crook and the flail were crossed on his chest, like royalty.

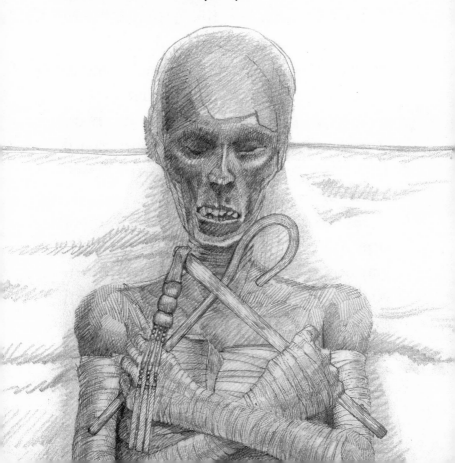

"Mom?" I called to her. My voice was high. "Mom?" I couldn't take my eyes off Neshi.

Finally she turned around and saw what I was staring at. In a flash she was at my side, looking at him intently.

"Cameron, how did this...what did you...weren't his arms...?" She couldn't finish her sentence. She glared at me like she thought somehow *I* had moved Neshi's arms.

"I didn't do anything, Mom. But I think you'd better leave the crook and flail right where they are. That's what Neshi wanted all along."

My mom was silent for the longest time. Finally she said, "All right, Cameron. For a while. But in one year, we'll have to return these artifacts to Egypt. The crook and flail belong to the government."

Oh, don't tell me that, Mom, I thought as the lump formed in the pit of my stomach again. I looked at Neshi. What would he do when my mom took the crook and flail away?

In the next instant, I knew for sure that Neshi could read my mind. Because he started to twitch, just a little. He was tightening his grip on the crook and flail.

I swallowed hard. Well, I told myself, at least it was a whole year away. Maybe I'd be able to sleep peacefully—until then. But sooner or later, I knew the time would come. Then, once again, the mummy would awake!

Megan Stine & H. William Stine have written more than sixty books together. Among them are many adventure, mystery, and humor titles for young readers. The Stines have lived all across the country, from San Francisco to New York City, but have as yet failed to discover a living mummy. At present this husband-and-wife team lives in Atlanta, Georgia, with their eleven-year-old son, Cody.

Peter Peebles is no stranger to mummies and scary monsters. He specializes in illustrations for covers of fantasy and science-fiction books. Many magazines have also featured this artist's work. Born and raised in Minneapolis, Minnesota, he now lives in Forest Hills, New York.